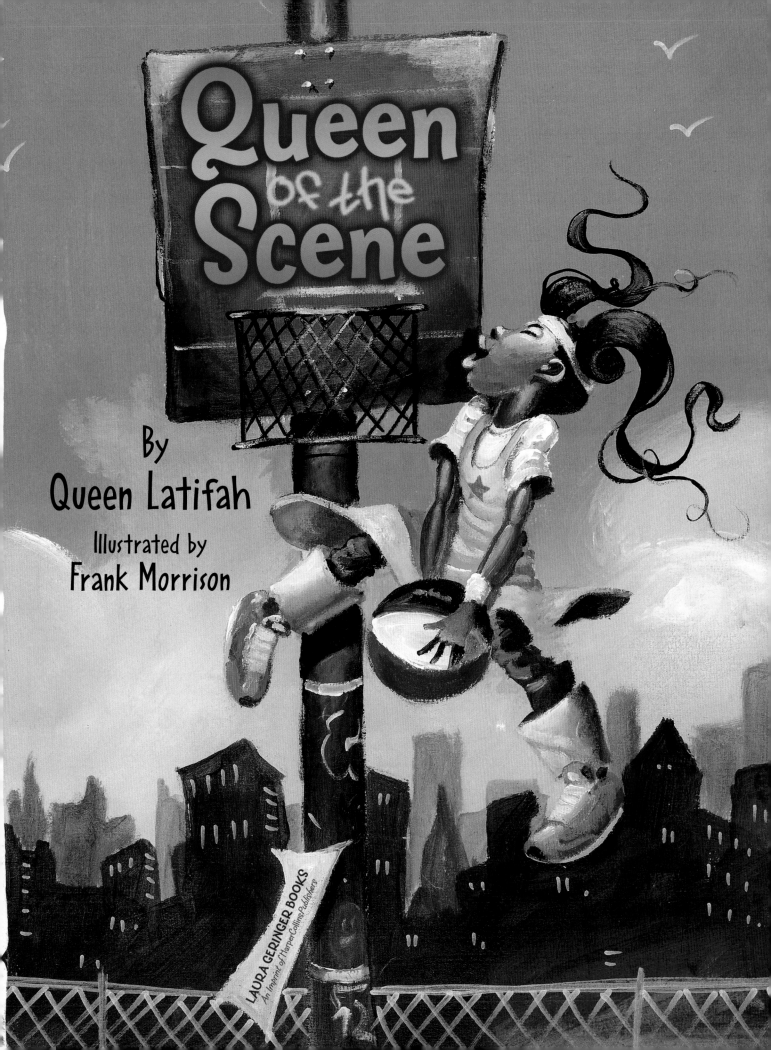

Queen of the Scene

By
Queen Latifah

Illustrated by
Frank Morrison

LAURA GERINGER BOOKS
An Imprint of HarperCollins Publishers

Library of Congress Cataloging-in-Publication Data
Latifah, Queen
  Queen of the scene / by Queen Latifah ; illustrated by Frank Morrison.— 1st ed.
    p.   cm.
  Summary: A self-confident young African-American girl explains why she is "queen of the scene" at the playground.
  ISBN-10: 0-06-077856-3 (trade bdg.) — ISBN-13: 978-0-06-077856-9 (trade bdg.)
  ISBN-10: 0-06-077857-1 (lib. bdg.) — ISBN-13: 978-0-06-077857-6 (lib. bdg.)
  [1. Self-perception—Fiction. 2. Self-confidence—Fiction. 3. Playgrounds-Fiction. 4. African Americans—Fiction. 5. Stories
in rhyme—Fiction.] I. Morrison, Frank, date, ill. II. Title.
PZ8.3.L34444Que 2006
[E]—dc22   2005018539
                                                                                                          CIP
                                                                                                          AC

Typography by Neil Swaab
1 2 3 4 5 6 7 8 9 10

First Edition

To my mother and all my teachers
—Q.L.

I dedicate this to my action heroes:
Nia, Nasir, Nyree, & Tyreek. Love, Daddy
—F.M.

I'm queen of the scene.
Baby, I'm a star!
I make games look easier
Than they are.

No stopping me at hop 'n' scotch—
Everybody comes to watch!

I'm as smooth as a machine,
I'm queen of the scene.

You don't want to race me—
I'm as fast as spinning dice.

And baby, I'm the best
When it comes to hand- and stickball—
I hit that ball so hard,
It can break a brick wall.

Or I can throw that same ball
Way up the highest slide,
Toss it up while coming down
And catch it in stride.

If you had a genie
That would grant you a wish,
You'd want to hoop like me—

There's no one who can beat
My speed-of-orbit feet—
I never take a rest,
'Cause baby, I'm the best.

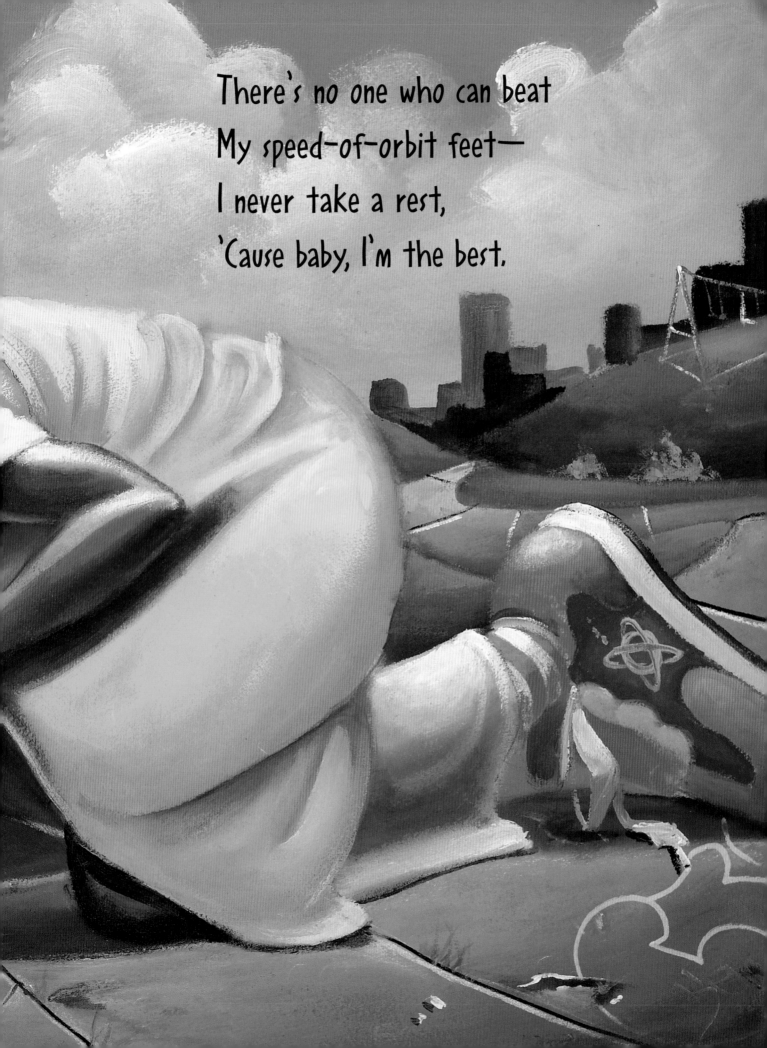

There's no one who can top me,
'Cause I got game.
No boy or girl can stop me
In any sport you name.

If you're standin' on the sidelines,
'Cause you don't have heart,
Then get yourself right back here,
'Cause I'm takin' your part.

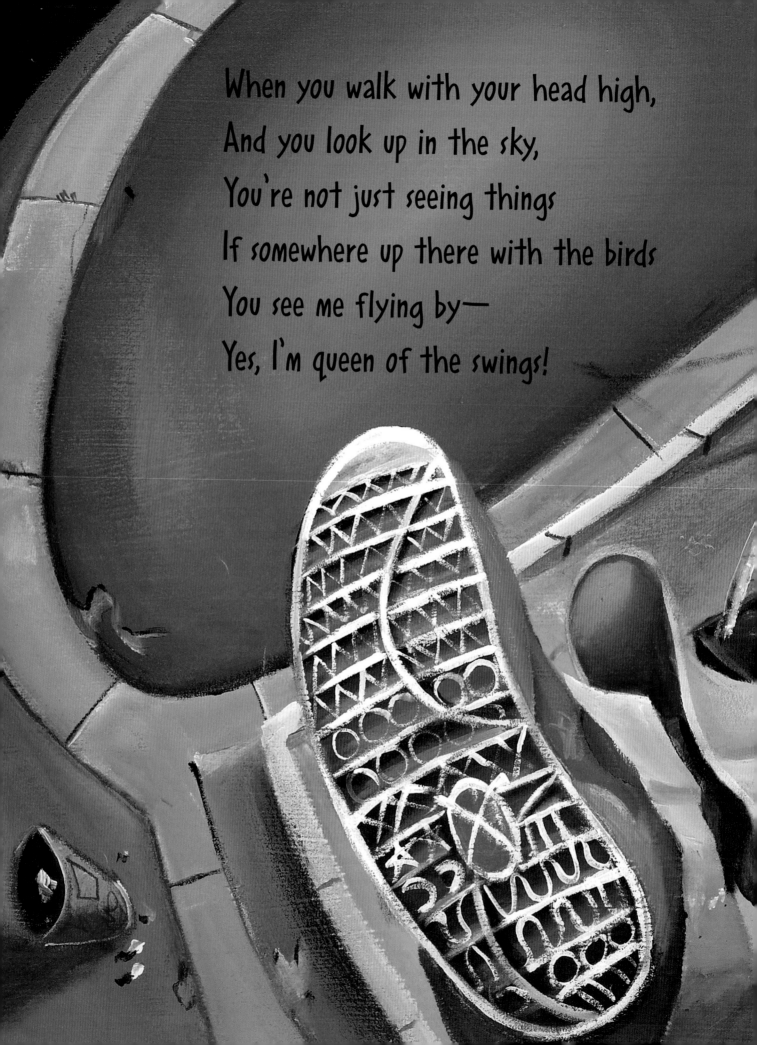

When you walk with your head high,
And you look up in the sky,
You're not just seeing things
If somewhere up there with the birds
You see me flying by—
Yes, I'm queen of the swings!

In any sandbox that I go to
Nobody can be mean.
My castles are the very best—
They're fit for a queen.

My double Dutch is hopping—
I can jump without stopping,
And I can shoot a skully top
Even while I'm shopping!

I can play just anything
From anywhere at all.

So girl, take pride—
Even if at first you fall
Keep giving it another try.
The queen in you walks tall.

Yes, I'm queen of the scene,
Ruler of the park,
But so long, it's getting late now—
I've got to be home by dark.